FROM FIRST TO LAST

By Dr. Seuss

CONTENTS

And to Think That I Saw
It on Mulberry Street

Oh, the Thinks You Can Think!

Oh, the Places You'll Go!

CARNIVAL

This omnibus edition first published 2005

HarperCollins*Publishers* Ltd
77-85 Fulham Palace Road
Hammersmith, London W6 8JB

Visit our website: www.harpercollinschildrensbooks.co.uk

ISBN 0 00 777544 X

Printed and bound in China by Imago

AND TO THINK THAT I SAW IT ON MULBERRY STREET

WHEN I leave home to walk to school,
Dad always says to me,
"Marco, keep your eyelids up
And see what you can see."

But when I tell him where I've been
And what I think I've seen,
He looks at me and sternly says,
"Your eyesight's much too keen.

"Stop telling such outlandish tales.
Stop turning minnows into whales."

Now, what can I say
When I get home today?

All the long way to school
And all the way back,
I've looked and I've looked
And I've kept careful track,
But all that I've noticed,
Except my own feet,
Was a horse and a wagon
On Mulberry Street.

That's nothing to tell of,
That won't do, of course . . .
Just a broken-down wagon
That's drawn by a horse.

That *can't* be my story. That's only a *start*.
I'll say that a ZEBRA was pulling that cart!
And that is a story that no one can beat,
When I say that I saw it on Mulberry Street.

Yes, the zebra is fine,
But I think it's a shame,
Such a marvellous beast
With a cart that's so tame.
The story would really be better to hear
If the driver I saw were a charioteer.
A gold and blue chariot's *something* to meet,
Rumbling like thunder down Mulberry Street!

No, it won't do at all . . .
A zebra's too small.

A reindeer is better;
He's fast and he's fleet,

And he'd look mighty smart
On old Mulberry Street.

Hold on a minute!
There's something wrong!

A reindeer hates the way it feels
To pull a thing that runs on wheels.

He'd be much happier, instead,
If he could pull a fancy sled.

Hmmmm . . . A reindeer and sleigh . .

Say—*any*one could think of *that*,
Jack or Fred or Joe or Nat—
Say, even Jane could think of *that*.

But it isn't too late to make one little change.
A sleigh and an ELEPHANT! *There's* something strange!

I'll pick one with plenty of power and size,
A blue one with plenty of fun in his eyes.
And then, just to give him a little more tone,
Have a Rajah, with rubies, perched high on a throne.

Say! That makes a story that *no one* can beat,
When I say that I saw it on Mulberry Street.

But now I don't know . . .
It still doesn't seem right.

An elephant pulling a thing that's so light
Would whip it around in the air like a kite.

But he'd look simply grand
With a great big brass band!

A band that's so good should have someone to hear it,
But it's going so fast that it's hard to keep near it.
I'll put on a trailer! I know they won't mind
If a man sits and listens while hitched on behind.

But now is it fair? Is it fair what I've done?
I'll bet those wagons weigh more than a ton.
That's really too heavy a load for *one* beast;
I'll give him some helpers. He needs two, at least.

But now what worries me is this . .
Mulberry Street runs into Bliss,

Unless there's something I can fix up,
There'll be an *awful* traffic mix-up!

It takes Police to do the trick,
To guide them through where traffic's thick —
It takes Police to do the trick.

They'll never crash now. They'll race at top speed
With Sergeant Mulvaney, himself, in the lead.

The Mayor is there
And he thinks it is grand,
And he raises his hat
As they dash by the stand.

The Mayor is there
And the Aldermen too,
All waving big banners
Of red, white and blue.

And that is a story that NO ONE can beat
When I say that I saw it on Mulberry Street!

With a roar of its motor an aeroplane appears
And dumps out confetti while everyone cheers.

And that makes a story that's really not bad!
But it still could be better. Suppose that I add . . . .

. . . A Chinaman
Who eats with sticks. . . .

A big Magician
Doing tricks . . .

A ten-foot beard
That needs a comb. . . .

No time for more,
I'm almost home.

I swung round the corner
And dashed through the gate,
I ran up the steps
And I felt simply GREAT!

FOR I HAD A STORY THAT **NO ONE** COULD BEAT!
AND TO THINK THAT I SAW IT ON MULBERRY STREET!

But Dad said quite calmly,
"Just draw up your stool
And tell me the sights
On the way home from school."

There was so much to tell, I JUST COULDN'T BEGIN!
Dad looked at me sharply and pulled at his chin.
He frowned at me sternly from there in his seat,
"Was there nothing to look at . . . no people to greet?
Did *nothing* excite you or make your heart beat?"

"Nothing," I said, growing red as a beet,
"But a plain horse and wagon on Mulberry Street."

Oh, the THINKS you Can Think!

You can
think up
some birds.
That's what you can do.
You can think about yellow
or think about blue . . .

You can think about red.
You can think about pink.
You can think up a horse.
Oh, the THINKS you can think!

Oh, the THINKS
you can think up
if only you try!

If you try,
you can think up
a GUFF going by.

And you don't have to stop.

You can think about SCHLOPP.

Schlopp. Schlopp. Beautiful schlopp.

Beautiful schlopp

with a cherry on top.

You can think about gloves.
You can think about SNUVS.

You can think a long time
about snuvs and their gloves.

You can think about
Kitty O'Sullivan Krauss
in her big balloon swimming pool
over her house.

Think of black water.

Think up a white sky.

Think up a boat.

Think of BLOOGS blowing by.

You can think about Night,
a night in Na-Nupp.
The birds are asleep
and the three moons are up.

You can think about Day,
a day in Da-Dake.
The water is blue
and the birds are awake.

Think! Think and wonder.
Wonder and think.
How much water
can fifty-five elephants drink?

You can wonder . . .

How long
is the tail
of a ZONG?

There are so many THINKS
that a Thinker can think!

Would you dare
yank a tooth
of the
RINK-RINKER-FINK?

And
what would
you do
if
you met
a JIBBOO?

Oh, the THINKS
you can think!

Think of
Peter the Postman
who crosses the ice
once every day—
and on Saturdays, twice.

THINK! You can think
any THINK
that you wish . . .

Think
a race
on a horse
on a ball
with a fish!

Think of Light.
Think of Bright.
Think of
Stairs in the Night.

THINK!

Think a ship.

Think up a long trip.

Go visit the VIPPER,

the Vipper of Vipp.

And left!

Think of Left!

And think about BEFT.
Why is it that beft
always go to the left?

And why is it
so many things
go to the Right?
You can think about THAT
until Saturday night.

Think left and think right
and think low and think high.
Oh, the THINKS you can
think up if only you try!

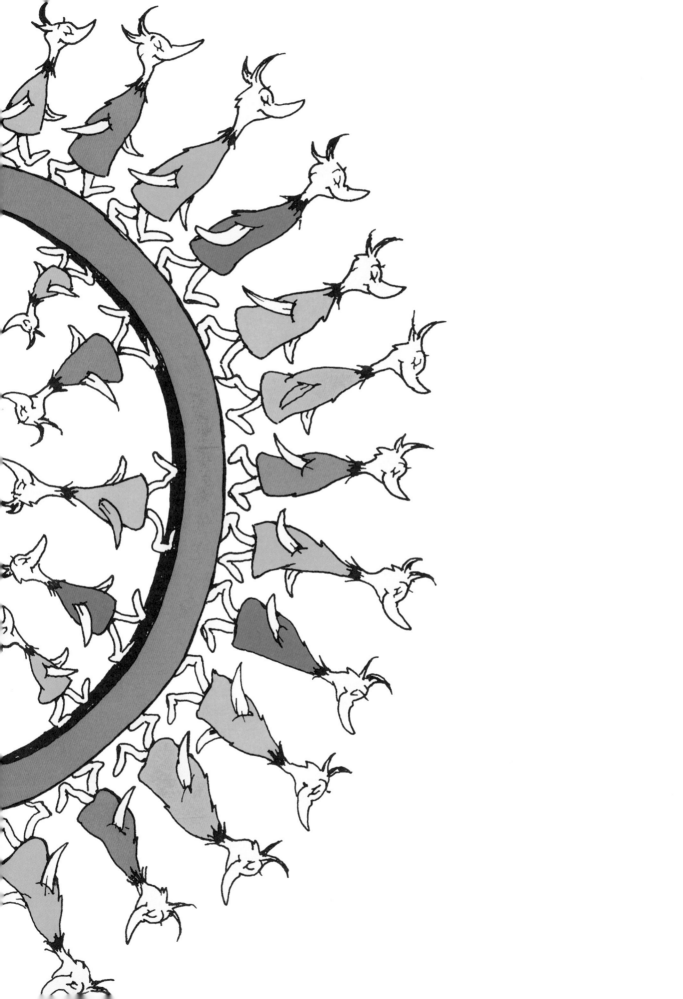

Oh, the Places You'll Go!

Congratulations!
Today is your day.
You're off to Great Places!
You're off and away!

You have brains in your head.
You have feet in your shoes.
You can steer yourself
any direction you choose.
You're on your own. And you know what you know.
And *YOU* are the guy who'll decide where to go.

You'll look up and down streets. Look 'em over with care.
About some you will say, "I don't choose to go there."
With your head full of brains and your shoes full of feet,
you're too smart to go down any not-so-good street.

And you may not find *any*
you'll want to go down.
In that case, of course,
you'll head straight out of town.

It's opener there
in the wide open air.

Out there things can happen
and frequently do
to people as brainy
and footsy as you.

And when things start to happen,
don't worry. Don't stew.
Just go right along.
You'll start happening too.

OH!
THE PLACES YOU'LL GO!

You'll be on your way up!
You'll be seeing great sights!
You'll join the high fliers
who soar to high heights.

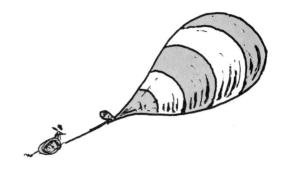

You won't lag behind, because you'll have the speed.
You'll pass the whole gang and you'll soon take the lead.
Wherever you fly, you'll be best of the best.
Wherever you go, you will top all the rest.

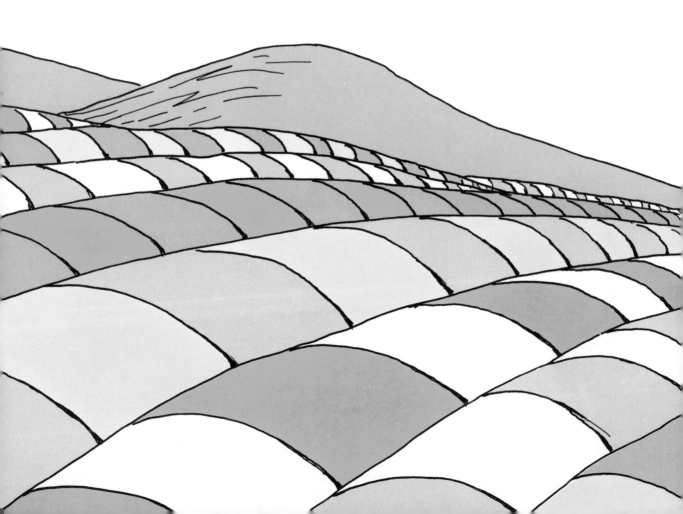

Except when you *don't*.
Because, sometimes, you *won't*.

I'm sorry to say so
but, sadly, it's true
that Bang-ups
and Hang-ups
can happen to you.

You can get all hung up
in a prickle-ly perch.
And your gang will fly on.
You'll be left in a Lurch.

You'll come down from the Lurch
with an unpleasant bump.
And the chances are, then,
that you'll be in a Slump.

And when you're in a Slump,
you're not in for much fun.
Un-slumping yourself
is not easily done.

You will come to a place where the streets are not marked.
Some windows are lighted. But mostly they're darked.
A place you could sprain both your elbow and chin!
Do you dare to stay out? Do you dare to go in?
How much can you lose? How much can you win?

And *IF* you go in, should you turn left or right . . .
or right-and-three-quarters? Or, maybe, not quite?
Or go around back and sneak in from behind?
Simple it's not, I'm afraid you will find,
for a mind-maker-upper to make up his mind.

You can get so confused
that you'll start in to race
down long wiggled roads at a break-necking pace
and grind on for miles across weirdish wild space,
headed, I fear, toward a most useless place.

The Waiting Place . . .

. . . for people just waiting.
    Waiting for a train to go
    or a bus to come, or a plane to go
    or the mail to come, or the rain to go
    or the phone to ring, or the snow to snow
    or waiting around for a Yes or No
    or waiting for their hair to grow.
    Everyone is just waiting.

Waiting for the fish to bite
or waiting for wind to fly a kite
or waiting around for Friday night
or waiting, perhaps, for their Uncle Jake
or a pot to boil, or a Better Break
or a string of pearls, or a pair of pants
or a wig with curls, or Another Chance.
Everyone is just waiting.

NO!
That's not for you!

Somehow you'll escape
all that waiting and staying.
You'll find the bright places
where Boom Bands are playing.

With banner flip-flapping,
once more you'll ride high!
Ready for anything under the sky.
Ready because you're that kind of a guy!

Oh, the places you'll go! There is fun to be done!
There are points to be scored. There are games to be won.
And the magical things you can do with that ball
will make you the winning-est winner of all.
Fame! You'll be famous as famous can be,
with the whole wide world watching you win on TV.

Except when they *don't*.
Because, sometimes, they *won't*.

I'm afraid that *some* times
you'll play lonely games too.
Games you can't win
'cause you'll play against you.

All Alone!
Whether you like it or not,
Alone will be something
you'll be quite a lot.

And when you're alone, there's a very good chance
you'll meet things that scare you right out of your pants.
There are some, down the road between hither and yon,
that can scare you so much you won't want to go on.

But on you will go
though the weather be foul.
On you will go
though your enemies prowl.
On you will go
though the Hakken-Kraks howl.
Onward up many
a frightening creek,
though your arms may get sore
and your sneakers may leak.

On and on you will hike.
And I know you'll hike far
and face up to your problems
whatever they are.

You'll get mixed up, of course,
as you already know.
You'll get mixed up
with many strange birds as you go.
So be sure when you step.
Step with care and great tact
and remember that Life's
a Great Balancing Act.
Just never forget to be dexterous and deft.
And *never* mix up your right foot with your left.

And will you succeed?
Yes! You will, indeed!
(98 and ¾ per cent guaranteed.)

KID, YOU'LL MOVE MOUNTAINS!

So . . .
be your name Buxbaum or Bixby or Bray
or Mordecai Ali Van Allen O'Shea,
you're off to Great Places!
Today is your day!
Your mountain is waiting.
So . . . *get on your way!*

Love you
too